SCHOOL SUPPLIES

selected by Lee Bennett Hopkins

A BOOK OF POEMS

illustrated by Renée Flower

8

10

12

& Schuster Books for Young Readers

For Rebecca Davis—
who supplies *me*
with enthusiasm.
—LBH

For Mr. Jimz
—RF

Contents

SCHOOL BUS by Lee Bennett Hopkins 8

from **PENCILS** by Carl Sandburg 11

NEW NOTEBOOK by Judith Thurman 12

BALLPOINT PEN by Lawrence Schimel 15

PAPER CLIPS by Rebecca Kai Dotlich 16

COMPASS by Georgia Heard 17

CLASSROOM GLOBE by Rebecca Kai Dotlich 18

LUNCH BAG by Chetra E. Kotzas 21

CRAYONS by Jane Yolen 22

POPSICLE STICKS AND GLUE by Leslie D. Perkins 25

A BOOK by Myra Cohn Livingston 26

MY WRITER'S NOTEBOOK by Brod Bagert 28

THE ERASER POEM by Louis Phillips 30

RUBBER BAND BRACELET by J. Patrick Lewis 31

from **PENCILS** by Carl Sandburg 33

HOMEWORK by Barbara Juster Esbensen 34

SCHOOL BUS

Lee Bennett Hopkins

This wide-awake
freshly-painted-yellow
school bus

readied for Fall

carries us all—

Sixteen boys—
Fourteen girls—

Thirty pairs of sleepy eyes

and

hundreds
upon
hundreds

of

school supplies.

from
PENCILS

Carl Sandburg

Pencils
telling where the wind comes from
open a story.

NEW NOTEBOOK

Judith Thurman

Lines
in a new notebook
run, even and fine,
like telephone wires
across a shadowy landscape.

With wet, black strokes
the alphabet settles between them,
comfortable as a flock of crows.

12

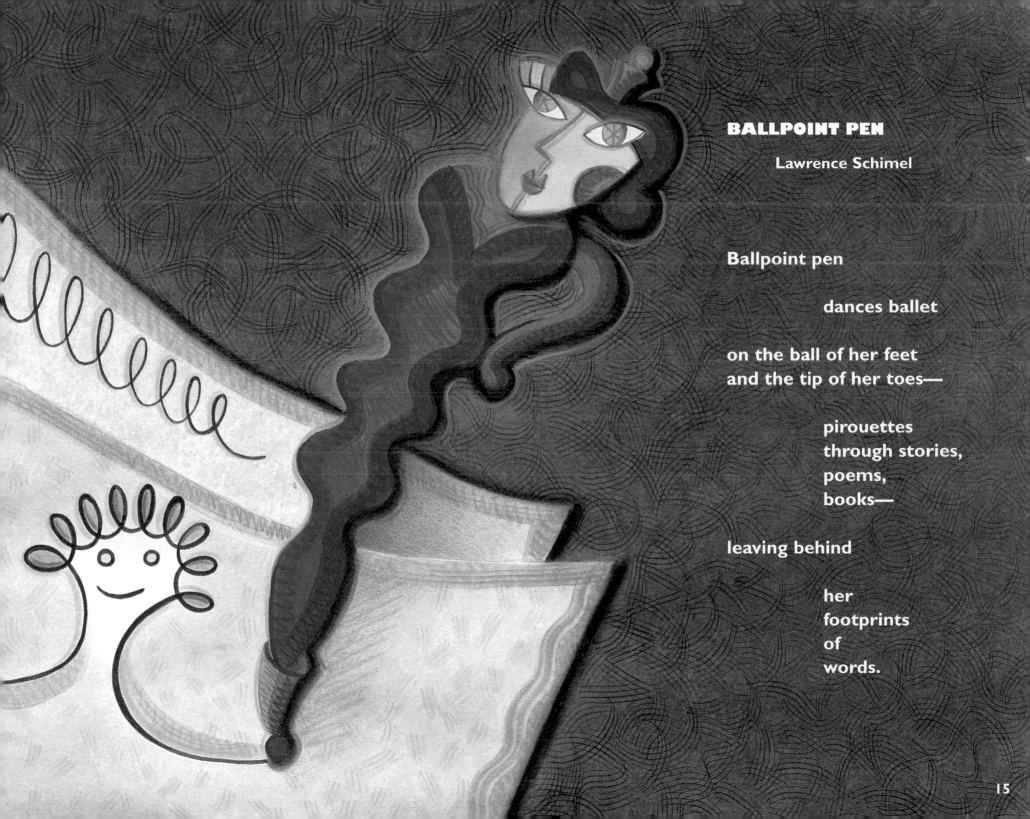

BALLPOINT PEN

Lawrence Schimel

Ballpoint pen

dances ballet

on the ball of her feet
and the tip of her toes—

pirouettes
through stories,
poems,
books—

leaving behind

her
footprints
of
words.

PAPER CLIPS

Rebecca Kai Dotlich

With tiny teeth
of tin
they take
one slender
breath
before they make
a move,
and then—
a silver pinch!

With jaws
no bigger
than an inch
these dragon grips
are small and slight—
but
conquer pages
with
one
bite!

16

COMPASS

Georgia Heard

It stands
on bright silver leg,
toe sharp and pointed.

The other leg draws
a perfect circle
like a skater gracefully
tracing
half a figure eight
on paper ice.

Its silver skirt above
measures out inches

    —two—three—four—

widening spheres
of mathematical perfection.

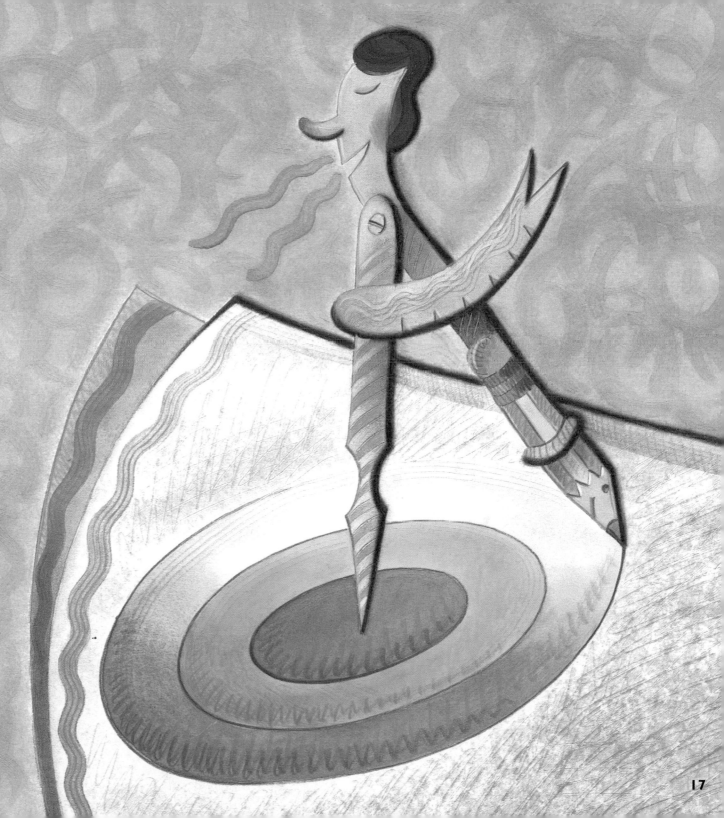

17

CLASSROOM GLOBE

Rebecca Kai Dotlich

Spinning, spinning,
round
and round,
a swirl of blue,
a whirl of brown;
mountain ranges,
oceans,
lakes,
islands,
foreign countries,
states.

Spinning, spinning,
stop!
Then linger.
Trace the earth
beneath
one finger.

18

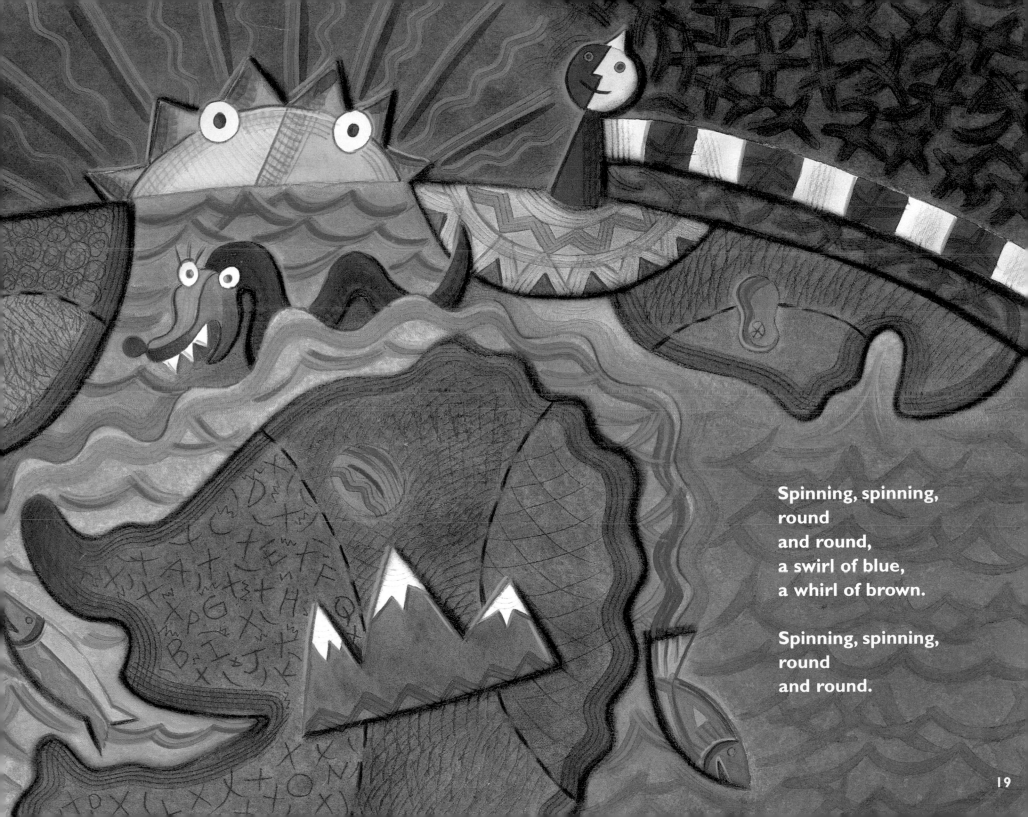

Spinning, spinning,
round
and round,
a swirl of blue,
a whirl of brown.

Spinning, spinning,
round
and round.

19

LUNCH BAG

Chetra E. Kotzas

Bulging
brown paper bag

hiding

one peanut butter sandwich,
round cookies, chocolate and chipped,
sweet bubbly pineapple juice
    with a twisty silver cap—

and

a little note that says:

    I LOVE YOU.

    GUESS WHO?

CRAYONS

Jane Yolen

This box contains a wash of blue sky,
spikes of green spring,
a circle of yellow sun,
triangle flames of orange and red.

It has the lime caterpillar
inching on a brown branch,
the shadow black in the center
of a grove of trees.

It holds my pink
and your chocolate
and her burnt sienna
and his ivory skin.

In it are all the colors of the world.

ALL
    the
       colors
          of
            the
              world.

POPSICLE STICKS AND GLUE

Leslie D. Perkins

We're building a village of popsicle sticks,
Just popsicle sticks and glue:

Houses and fences, sidewalks and streets,
A school and a library, too;
Museums, churches, temples, shops,
A playground, a park, and a zoo.

Isn't it wonderful what we can do
With popsicle sticks and a new tube of glue?

25

A BOOK

Myra Cohn Livingston

Closed, I am a mystery.
Open, I will always be
a friend with whom you think and see.

Closed, there's nothing I can say.
Open, we can dream and stray
to other worlds, far and away.

MY WRITER'S NOTEBOOK

Brod Bagert

It's a three-hole spiral notebook,
A hundred pages
With blue lines
That await my words:

Diamond Search

My life lies before me
Like the bed of a shallow river.
My fingers sift sand and gravel
For the rough diamonds that lie hidden.
And as I find them
I put them in this notebook.
I write… I cut… I polish…
And they shine.

My words on an empty page
In an ordinary notebook,
The silver setting for the jewels of my life.

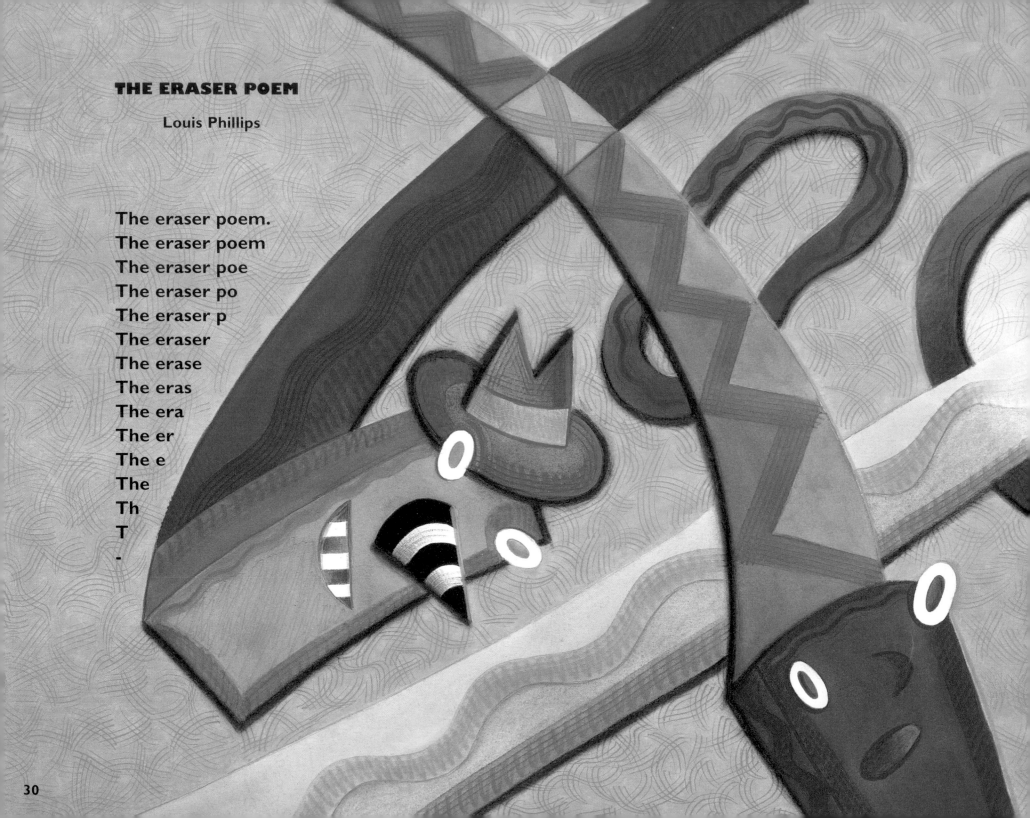

THE ERASER POEM

Louis Phillips

The eraser poem.
The eraser poem
The eraser poe
The eraser po
The eraser p
The eraser
The erase
The eras
The era
The er
The e
The
Th
T
-

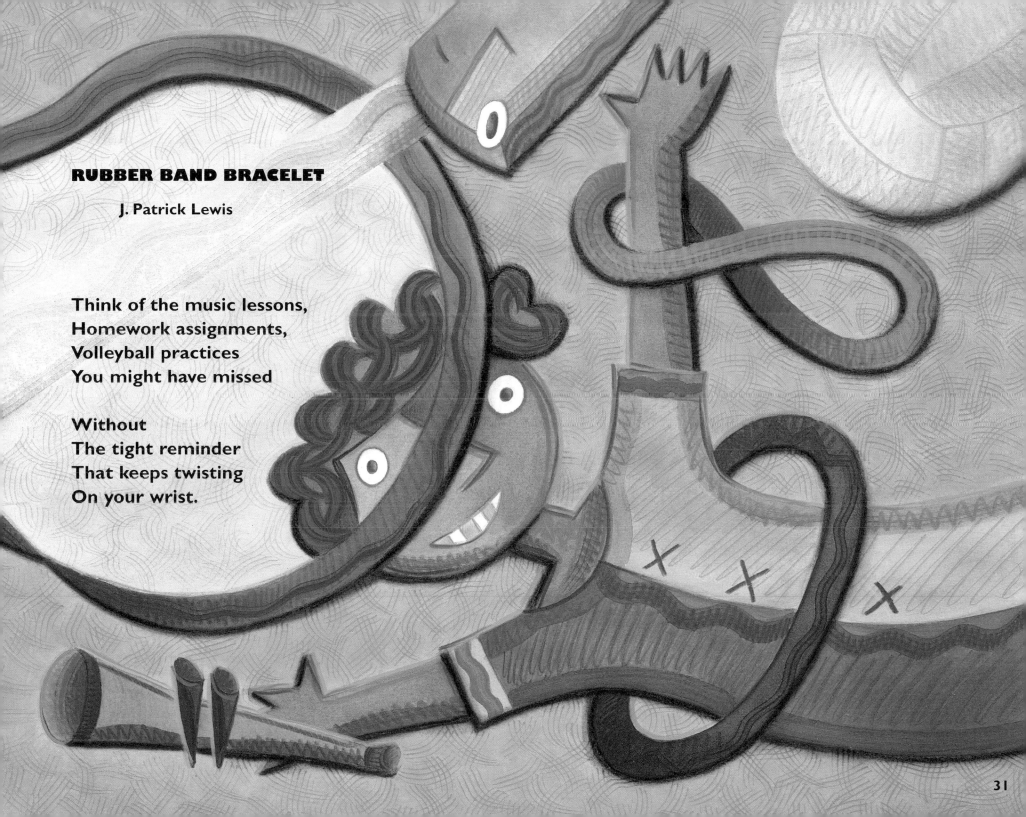

RUBBER BAND BRACELET

J. Patrick Lewis

Think of the music lessons,
Homework assignments,
Volleyball practices
You might have missed

Without
The tight reminder
That keeps twisting
On your wrist.

31

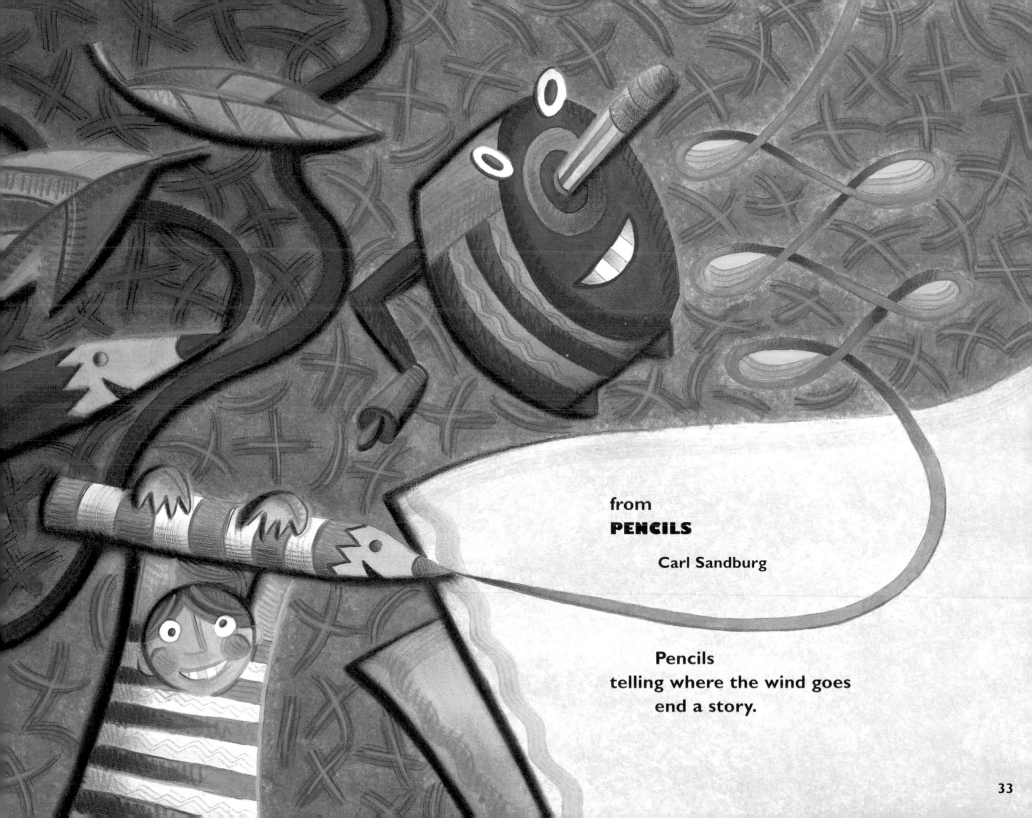

from
PENCILS

Carl Sandburg

Pencils
telling where the wind goes
end a story.

33

HOMEWORK

Barbara Juster Esbensen

It rustles   it
shifts   with no wind
in the room to
move it
Listen!
The blank white
paper
needs your attention

"Where are the words?"
it whispers
"I'm lonesome
for words and circles
and
spelling your name and
assignments"

34

Put your hand on the paper
to calm it   Pick up
your pen   Say
"Paper   I'm here
when you need me!"

Begin

ACKNOWLEDGMENTS

Thanks are due to the following for works reprinted herein:
Brod Bagert for "My Writer's Notebook." Used by permission of the author, who controls all rights. / Curtis Brown, Ltd. for "School Bus" by Lee Bennett Hopkins. Copyright © 1996 by Lee Bennett Hopkins. "Crayons" by Jane Yolen. Copyright © 1994 by Jane Yolen. Reprinted by permission of Curtis Brown, Ltd. / Rebecca Kai Dotlich for "Classroom Globe" and "Paper Clips." Used by permission of the author, who controls all rights. / Harcourt Brace and Company for excerpts from "Pencils" in *Smoke and Steel* by Carl Sandburg. Copyright 1920 by Harcourt Brace and Company and renewed 1948 by Carl Sandburg. Reprinted by permission of Harcourt Brace and Company. / HarperCollins Publishers for "Homework" from *Who Shrank My Grandmother's House?: Poems of Discovery* by Barbara Juster Esbensen. Copyright © 1992 by Barbara Juster Esbensen. Reprinted by permission of HarperCollins Publishers. / Georgia Heard for "Compass." Used by permission of the author, who controls all rights. / Chetra E. Kotzas for "Lunch Bag." Used by permission of the author, who controls all rights. / J. Patrick Lewis for "Rubber Band Bracelet." Used by permission of the author, who controls all rights. / Leslie D. Perkins for "Popsicle Sticks and Glue." Used by permission of the author, who controls all rights. / Louis Phillips for "The Eraser Poem." Used by permission of the author, who controls all rights. / Marian Reiner for "A Book" from *My Head Is Red and Other Riddle Rhymes* by Myra Cohn Livingston. Copyright © 1990 by Myra Cohn Livingston. "New Notebook" from *Flashlight and Other Poems* by Judith Thurman. Copyright © 1976 by Judith Thurman. Reprinted by permission of Marian Reiner for the authors. / Lawrence Schimel for " Ballpoint Pen." Used by permission of the author, who controls all rights.

SIMON & SCHUSTER BOOKS FOR YOUNG READERS

An imprint of Simon & Schuster Children's Publishing Division

1230 Avenue of the Americas, New York, New York 10020

Text copyright © 1996 by Lee Bennett Hopkins

Illustrations copyright © 1996 by Renée Flower

Simon & Schuster Books for Young Readers is a trademark of Simon & Schuster.

Book design by Lucille Chomowicz

The text for this book is set in Gill Sans Bold

The illustrations are rendered in watercolor and colored pencil

Printed and bound in the United States of America

First Edition

10 9 8 7 6 5 4 3 2 1

Library of Congress Cataloging-in-Publication Data

School supplies : a book of poems / selected by Lee Bennett Hopkins ;

illustrated by Renée Flower.

p.   cm.

1. Schools—Furniture, equipment, etc.—Juvenile poetry.

2. Children's poetry, American. I. Hopkins, Lee Bennett.

PS595.S34S36 1996

811.008'0355—dc20 94-38667

ISBN 0-689-80497-0